SELLING SHORT

Other CV-2 Books by Raymund Eich

Stone Chalmers
The Progress of Mankind
The Greater Glory of God
To All High Emprise Consecrated

The Confederated Worlds
Take the Shilling
Operation Iago
A Bodyguard of Lies

Novels
The Blank Slate
New California

Short Novels
The ALECS Quartet

Collections
The First Voyages: The Complete Science Fiction Stories
1998-2012

SELLING SHORT

Raymund Eich

CV-2 Books • Houston

This is a work of fiction. All the characters and events portrayed in this book are fictitious, and any resemblance to real people, living or dead, or any known events is purely coincidental.

SELLING SHORT © 2011 Raymund Eich

Cover art: Sun: NASA, `http://solarscience.msfc.nasa.gov/surface.shtml` (NASA does not endorse this use of the image.)
Spaceship: © Algol I Dreamstime.com
Starfield: © Ryhor Bruyeu I Dreamstime.com
Cover design, book design, and aircraft carrier logo are copyrights, trademarks, or trade dress of CV-2 Books.

First CV-2 Books trade paperback edition: December 2018

10 9 8 7 6 5 4 3 2 1

SELLING SHORT

The freighter *Coronado*'s conference room had a hardwood floor and leather chairs. Reflected light smeared over the polished ebony table as Marqus sat. No one else had arrived yet. His hands slid over the wood, and six hundred yards below the floor the ship's fusion drive rumbled. He smiled a giddy grin. New Liberia, his home, five space habitats orbiting Saturn's moon Titan, lay two hours behind the ship. He lived his own life now, not the one his parents wanted him to live.

Unfamiliar bodies and voices flowed into the room. The chair to his right squeaked, and he turned to see Raveena. "Hi, Marqus," she said. "Welcome aboard."

"Thanks." In the flesh, she looked like the avatar she'd shown in his Virtual job interview a week before. South Asian, Raveena had a long narrow nose and thin lips. She wore a navy-blue jumper and straight black hair in a pageboy cut.

"Settled in?" she asked.

He nodded, and glanced up as more people entered the room. "I've been in my cabin a few hours."

"All unpacked?"

"One of your robots unpacked my things." The ship had fifteen robots, like pygmy centaurs with tiger-stripe plastic skin, three feet long and two feet to the shoulder. They performed service and maintenance tasks; the one that helped Marqus had climbed the walls on its gecko feet to hang his clothes bags.

"You must have brought a lot, if it took you so long."

"Not really...." Sweat trickled on his nape. In his cabin, he'd installed and primed a censorship program Captain Garcia had purchased: *Sun, helium, Venus...* He couldn't tell her that.

"Have you met everyone?"

"In Virtual, yes." Eight other people sat around the table, and chatted amongst themselves. Sonoma, a pale woman, talked with Naseem, a slender Arab. The latter glanced at Marqus, with a look his ancestors had fixed on black men during slave raids centuries ago. Marqus turned away, but watched Sonoma through one of the ship's cameras. She had high cheekbones and straight red hair. He'd never seen a woman like her. She leaned toward Naseem, and parted her full lips in a shared laugh. "Some people don't resemble their avatars."

At the table's head, the Chinese man, navigator Xi Qen, and Annike Olson, the financial officer, flanked Captain Garcia. The captain laughed at someone's joke, then stood and cleared his throat. Conversations died down. Garcia stood six-feet-two, with brown eyes under thick eyebrows. His van dyke beard emphasized his jaw. "First, has everyone met our new officer trainee, Marqus du Bois? We hired him at New Liberia."

Nods ringed the table. Olson folded her arms. She'd been aloof in his interview, and he couldn't tell why. Garcia looked at him and raised an eyebrow. –Say something,– the captain said privately.

"I'll administer the ship's computer system," Marqus said. "I look forward to working with you." He couldn't think of anything else, and closed his mouth.

–Thanks, Marqus,– Garcia said. "The second order of business involves our destination and cargo."

Murmurs bubbled, and Raveena leaned forward. "Why *did* you refit the *Coronado* with insulation? Why are we taking methane to colonies around Neptune? The profit margin's thin."

Garcia grinned. "I'll be happy to tell you everything." He looked around the table. "But first, you have to consent to running your outgoing messages through a censor program."

The murmurs doubled. "Censorship?" Ludmilla said. Glitter on her eyelids flashed when she blinked. "We have a right to privacy!"

"Your right to privacy ends where ship's security begins," Garcia said, but then softened his voice. "We won't record what you say. The program will flag messages containing certain words, and I'll review only those messages before they go out. I don't want to do this, but if certain parties in the solar system knew our plan, we could be in trouble. You'll have to trust me." Marqus sensed everyone agree.

"Now Raveena, you asked why we're hauling methane to a gas giant? Simple. We're not. I sold it before we took delivery." Garcia's gaze darted from face to face. "Everyone get up to speed on terraforming Venus."

The ship's network fed thoughts to Marqus like a forgotten memory returning to mind. Before humans arrived, hot carbon dioxide smothered the planet. To terraform Venus, people first had to remove the atmosphere. He superimposed a hologram of the planet over his real vision. Venus appeared as a fuzzy, striped yellow ball above the conference table. It hung in the shadow of a rotating disc eight thousand miles across. Dubbed the SPF-Infinity, the disc blocked sunlight and allowed the atmosphere to cool. Humans lived in cities along the disc's rim. When cold enough, the atmosphere would rain on the surface, and then freeze into a dry ice shell half a mile deep. Unaided, though, cooling would take centuries.

To speed the process, the Venus Climatology Ministry had built a cooling tower, Beanstalk-1. Five hundred miles high, the tower jutted through Venus' clouds. Marqus looked for it, and rotated the Virtual hologram until the tower's tip, marked by a beacon, came into view. Though huge, the cooling tower operated on a simple principle: liquid helium flowed down the tower's inner wall, and near the surface atmospheric heat turned it into gas. Helium vapor then floated up the tower's annulus, radiated its heat into space, and became liquid again to restart the cycle. Beanstalk-2 was under construction, and radicals in the Venus parliament demanded a third.

"It all comes down to helium," Garcia said. "There isn't any in Venus' atmosphere, so the government has to import it. Some helium always leaks out, and the second tower will double demand. Now, when demand goes up–"

The planet's image vanished, and up popped a chart of helium prices at the market in Ishtar, the largest city on SPF-Infinity's rim. So far this year, the price had gone up five-fold; it now traded at two thousand sols per ton.

"Two thousand sols a ton!" Garcia said. "The *Coronado* can carry 180,000 tons. Do the math!"

Marqus had hired on for 2.0% of the ship's profits. His jaw sagged. He would earn over seven million sols! He could retire after one journey! They all could. Naseem grinned, and Sonoma glanced at the captain with a satisfied look.

"It's not so simple," Xi said. Concern marred his face. "The price is up because of the Preservationists. Ever since their hard-line faction took over...."

"They'll boycott the *Coronado*, and each of us, for the rest of our lives," Raveena said.

Heinrich palmed his shaven, tattooed scalp. "We won't have a rest of our lives. Between here and Venus, bulk helium is only found in Jupiter's atmosphere. Surrounded by Preservationist settlements on its moons! If we try to take helium, they'll gun us down!"

"Another gas giant?" Naseem asked. "No, the Presers could intercept us on the way to Venus."

Marqus' eyes went wide, and he blinked at the captain with sudden respect.

"You've all missed it," Garcia said. "We're going to the sun."

"We'll burn up!" Heinrich said.

Garcia shook his head. "That's why I refitted the *Coronado* with ceramic insulator all around the hull. It'll stop radiation and slow heat absorption. We'll have two weeks before the ship's interior gets too hot." His smile had a manic edge. "We can mine helium from the sun."

Ludmilla's brow furrowed. "The photosphere is 10,000 degrees, and it gets hotter further in!"

"We won't go further in," Garcia said. "There's enough helium outside the photosphere for us to fill the hold in nine or ten days. The gas out there, in the chromosphere, is also less dense, so it'll be a gentler ride. It can be done." He leaned forward, fists on the table. "This will be our most profitable trip ever."

The ship accelerated at point-two gee, enough to keep Marqus' soles on the deck. New Liberia's spinning-wheel space habitats soon faded from naked eyesight against Titan's orange clouds. Abstractly, he'd known New Liberia was insular and isolated; he'd seen how tiny it was from a distance in Virtuals; but seeing it for real, as an image derived from photons reflected off atoms and not neurons induced to fire within his visual cortex, made his cheeks clammy. Even if he went back, he'd never think of New Liberia the same way.

The *Coronado* had filed a flight plan, destination Neptune, with a gravitational slingshot around the sun to gain more speed. In his mind's eye, Marqus saw the flight plan, a blue line, turn yellow as the ship crept along it. At the sun, their true flight plan, a red line, curled off and wound itself around Sol. It wouldn't be easy–the orbital insertion into the sun's chromosphere required the *Coronado* to decelerate at three gees for a day and a half–but the ship could do it.

Should he call his parents? Mother would be worried, but Father would try to put doubts in his head. *Those ofays and oreos will never treat you as an equal*, Marqus imagined his father say. He had to prove himself first. He got to work.

The prior computer administrator, Lorelei, had left the ship six months before. The public memory had grown sloppy since then, littered with file fragments and backed up behind schedule, if at all. Between cleaning up the computer system and absorbing technical manuals, he worked late the first few nights. When he woke, though, deep in his third night aboard with the lights in his cabin still on and murky thoughts of transmitter hardware in his mind, he knew he had to do more than work.

So he sought out his crew mates. Though he felt uneasy at first, the crew's friendliness showed him most people didn't fit into stereotypes. He liked Raveena, despite her fondness for martial arts and role-playing Virtuals with dancing elephants and six-armed blue gods. He played chess with Heinrich and racquetball with the captain. Ludmilla introduced him to golf in Virtual. He felt foolish at first, in long pants and spiked shoes, but legends of Tiger Woods and Albert Nkomo buoyed him. By the eighteenth tee, he wanted to try again.

The person he most wanted to meet, though, was the least accessible: Sonoma. Her hazel eyes made his heart pound and sweat meander down his back. He told his software assistant to calm his heart rate and deepen his voice when he met her. As soon as he next saw her, though, he felt certain she saw what he'd done and she'd think less of him for it. He stammered through the conversation, and walked away with hot cheeks. He wondered if his mother were right about white women's witchery.

He avoided Naseem, and both Xi and Olson remained aloof. The navigator spent his free time in his cabin. The whine of precision tools and the sweet stink of hot polymers sneaked into the corridor.

"What's his hobby?" Marqus asked Raveena as they passed Xi's door.

She shrugged. "He tinkers. He never socialized much, but he's been a hermit since his wife left."

"Lorelei?" he asked. Raveena nodded. "Why'd she go?"

"She became a Preservationist. Filed for divorce and left for Callisto. And she took their daughter, which bothers me the most."

"How so?" Marqus asked. "I don't know much about Preservationists."

"They think human beings are a cancer on the Solar System," she said. His software assistant told him cancer was a disease. "It's a bad enough life for an adult to choose: a tiny apartment and meditating on the beauty of ice and rocks all day. Inflicting that on a child…" Marqus felt sudden sympathy for Xi.

Olson, on the other hand, played a strong role in the ship's social life, but Marqus felt small whenever he met her. Late one night, he stepped into the main corridor of the crew deck and almost collided with her as she jogged.

"I'm sorry," he said, and shuffled to the side.

She jogged in place. Her sweat masked the dead odor of white people. "Don't mention it." Olson's blue eyes stared without seeing; her software assistant had spoken through her mouth. She took a step.

It had been five days. He had to speak. "Ms. Olson?"

Her body turned. "Call me Annike."

"Have I offended you?"

"No," came from her mouth.

His father, face stern, had told him he'd come crawling home. Dread filled Marqus. "Do you dislike me because I'm black?"

Annike stopped jogging, and muscles flowed in her face. "What!? What gave you that idea?"

"You don't want me on board. I don't know why."

She shrugged. "Marqus, it's nothing personal, but we shouldn't have hired you right now. We don't need a sixth officer trainee. You're not worth the cost."

"Your computer system's a mess–"

"You worked for New Liberia traffic control, right? Computer glitches could crash ships. Our system's good enough. I've handled it for six months. Pardon me?"

He nodded. Her face reset, and she jogged away. Her body veered around a robot carrying a laundry bag on its back. It glanced at her with doting eyes. He watched the small of Annike's back, where sweat darkened her gray sportbra, until the curving corridor took her out of sight. His chin lifted. They didn't need him? He'd prove her wrong! He belonged on the *Coronado*. He knew it.

On the twelfth day out from New Liberia, the ship accelerated past Jupiter. Sol lay a week away, and it looked to be a long week.

A news item crossed the solar system. The Presers demanded a ban on all helium deliveries to Venus. They weren't bluffing, either. The Presers had an outpost on Uranus' moon Desdemona. A warship from the outpost chased a helium harvester leaving the gas giant's atmosphere, destroyed the harvester's fusion drive, then arrested the crew. The Venus Defense Ministry launched a squadron on maneuvers to the asteroid belt. Helium's cash price jumped to 6872¼ sols a ton, and the futures contract for next-month deliveries broke six thousand.

Garcia invited the crew to the conference room. Robots circled the room with bottles of rhiesling and pinot noir. Marqus smiled wide to jolt their pleasure circuits each time they filled his glass. Virtual vases with yellow hydrangeas stood around the room. Dance music played in the crew's heads, and a few crewmen's bodies jerked to the rhythm.

"Come celebrate! We're rich!" Garcia made avatars appear to expand the crowd, and mingled with a glint in his eyes.

After a while, Marqus talked with Raveena while she drank. "The captain's excited," Marqus said.

"His potential profit is a half-billion sols. I'd be bouncing off the ceiling." She held his gaze for a moment, then looked away.

"So why isn't Annike happy?" She stood at the doorway, her back to the jamb, and talked with Naseem and Sonoma. Maybe now he could talk to Sonoma. Marqus went over, and Raveena followed.

"We should sell a futures contract now." Annike spoke with exaggerated drunken care. "Prices can't stay this high. The profit takers will act. We could sell 150,000 tons for next-month delivery and lock in a good profit."

"Good?" Naseem said. "That's a billion sols! Why doesn't the captain–"

"He'll make up some bullshit about the Presers finding us. But that's not it. He's deep in debt."

Marqus couldn't speak for a moment. –How can she air his secrets like that!–

–She's letting the wine talk for her.– Raveena frowned. Through the thoughtspace, Marqus sensed she talked with Annike.

Annike shook her head. "No, he's behind on payments, and he took shaky loans to pay for the insulation–"

Garcia must have been eavesdropping. He strode toward them, his hand clenched white around a bottle's neck. His gaze swept over them, and Marqus quailed. "Despite what Annike might want, we will not sell a futures contract. First, we'd have to disable the censor program to send the sell order."

Annike reeled, then pressed her lips together. "We code the message."

"You think they don't have agents among the Venus futures brokers? Second, we'd be fools to sell now. The price is still climbing."

"Rey, there will be profit taking–"

"And the Presers will blow helium haulers apart. We're fine." Garcia glared, his pupils wide. "Come with me." He hooked her arm and led her out.

Naseem squinted at their backs. "Damn, isn't a billion sols enough for him?"

"He's right," Marqus said.

The Arab rolled his eyes. "He's not here. You don't have to suck up."

Sonoma turned to Marqus. "You think he's right?"

Naseem brooded with sudden jealousy. Good. Sonoma's hazel eyes made him light-headed, but he managed to speak. "I can understand her desire to cash in, but the captain's right about security."

Naseem shook his head. "A billion sols is worth the risk." To Sonoma he said, "The party's fading. Let's go."

"Sure," she said, but on the way out she held Marqus' gaze for a moment. He stared after her until Raveena cleared her throat.

"Marqus, can we talk?"

"Sure. What about?"

"I'm not normally so forthright." She bowed her head, and a blush bloomed on her cheeks. "I'd like to date you." She looked up with her eyes wide and hopeful.

His mouth opened, but he couldn't smile. Why not? Despite her skinny rear, he found her attractive enough. Friendly, too. What held him back? His parents' slanders of "dotheads?" His hopes about Sonoma? Not even that….

His software assistant fed a thought to his consciousness. Raveena simply wasn't feminine enough. Her baggy jumpsuits and *jeet kune do* didn't appeal to him. "I'm sorry. I like you, but not romantically."

"You could if you wanted to." She shrugged. "But if you don't, your loss."

Sure, he could reconfigure his mind. But he might lose something he liked about himself. Though the outlines were usually clear, reconfiguring was always unpredictable. She half-smiled–with her mouth and cheeks, but not her eyes. "Thanks for understanding," he said, though he wasn't sure she did. She soon said goodnight.

Tensions, both in the solar system and on board, wound tighter the next few days. The Presers ordered a squadron toward Venus. Premier Zhao of the East Asian Federation of Peoples' Republics invited diplomats from both sides to a meeting in ten days. Yet most voices in the solar system expected war.

Garcia and Annike argued in their cabin; the disagreement about profit taking revealed deeper clefts in their relationship. Arguments over money and ship management leaked through the door.

The strain on board eased, though, the last day before they entered the sun, as they passed ten million miles from Earth: on Ishtar's trading floor, helium's cash price reached eight thousand. Annike and the captain smiled and touched each other in public. Too, Marqus' friendship with Raveena grew more relaxed, and he found himself glad.

A few hours before the orbital burn, Marqus looked through the ship's forward cameras as Sol grow larger. The sun washed out the background stars, and soon, details resolved. Glowing gas wisps arced ten thousand miles over blotchy red sunspots. The *Coronado*'s surface temperature climbed. Marqus sensed the hull distort as the helium collectors moved into position. Time for the orbital burn.

In the crew lounge, tanks extruded from the walls and swung up their lids. Sonoma climbed into a tank on the far side of the room. During the burn, the crew would be confined to Virtual for a day and a half; perhaps he could talk to her then. Marqus climbed into his tank. Umbilicals slithered to his face and groin to provide air, water, food, and waste removal. His attention left his body before crash gel filled the tank.

He emerged in a public Virtual simulating the ship's interior. He stepped through the gel and the lid into the Virtual lounge. Heinrich and Raveena's avatars stood there. "We're going to the stern," she said. "Join us if you want."

He thought about Sonoma, and realized she had entered a private Virtual. His mood fell. "Sure."

They drifted through the floor. The bulkhead between the crew deck and the fuel tanks crawled up their legs, torsos, heads. Marqus stuck out his tongue and grimaced at the taste.

Inside the tank, he shivered at cold vacuum. A hundred yards below lay a dark surface like a black sand beach. Deuterium pellets. Abruptly, the pellets rustled toward them. The captain had cut off the thrust.

Marqus felt queasy for a few seconds as the ship swung around and aimed its stern forward for the deceleration burn. Through the deut pellets he glimpsed the fusion drive's injector, six hundred yards across the tank. The pellets crawled over them like a thousand frozen cat tongues. Heinrich said, "I hope Garcia's right about the insulation."

Marqus remembered the specs he'd learned. "If the pellets melt, we'll be out of fuel."

"If they vaporize," Raveena said, "the pressure would tear the ship apart."

They drifted toward the drive. The deut's metallic smell made him gag–he turned it off, replaced it with hydrangea fragrance. After a minute, they neared the fuel tank's aft bulkhead. Marqus pulled himself through the hull, and it solidified under his feet. He stood on the stern and gaped.

The sun occupied half the sky, like a molten gold wall too tall to climb. A prominence arced around them. His software assistant dimmed the brightness, which made Raveena and Heinrich's avatars shadowy wraiths. Convection roiled the sun's surface, and the simulated heat made him sweat. The size of it made his breath ragged. He shut his eyes and turned his head. His inner eyelids blazed bright green. His software assistant steeled him against the sight, and he reopened his eyes.

A hatch opened twenty yards away, and a blur shot out. Marqus glimpsed a curved metal probe, three yards high. The probe streaked with reflected sunlight for a few seconds, and then vanished along their flight path. The probe would coast towards Neptune and transmit false telemetry to traffic controllers along the way. It should buy them a week before the Preservationists realized where the Coronado had gone. Marqus watched the sun's limb for a last glimpse of the probe, but then the sun moved around the stern's rim and he felt like he'd be thrown into it. He shut his eyes again until his assistant made the feeling seem normal.

Then the fusion drive kicked in, and flung helium out the stern at ten million miles a minute; but the exhaust appeared as a pale wisp. It would take 35 hours to slow the ship to the sun's orbital velocity. Thirty-five hours? Marqus imagined for an irrational moment it would take forever, considering how weak the ship's drive seemed in comparison to the fusion reactor looming over them.

The burn did end on schedule, and once the crew grew accustomed to the *Coronado*'s reorientation (instead of walking them around in a circle, the main corridor was now a treadmill, with doors on the floor and ceiling, and the furnishings in their cabins retracted and re-extruded ninety degrees away), they settled into a routine. The helium collectors whined as they pulled in the sun's hot gases, mostly hydrogen and helium, and threw the hydrogen overboard. Eleven tons of helium a minute, sixteen thousand tons a day, filled the hold. A little slower than expected, but fast enough. They would top off the hold sometime on day twelve. The number popped into Marqus' head: based on the last helium price quote they'd received, he earned 22 sols per second.

To earn it, he only had to sweat. The ten thousand degree heat outside began to transfer through the ceramic, and the temperature crept up, two degrees a day. Sweat stained their shirts, and by the fourth day, Heinrich walked around shirtless. His bare belly stretched tight his shorts' waistband. By day seven, the ship's robots fumbled to put empty water bottles in their trash bags. Marqus frowned. The robots usually had good coordination. Were they heat-drunk?

That night, Marqus realized Naseem wanted to talk to the crew. The Arab had set up a Virtual inversion of the conference room, with a parquet tabletop and ebony floor. Naseem's avatar stood at the head of the table, arms folded. The others looked as puzzled as Marqus felt. –What's going on?– He asked Raveena.

She shrugged.

The room filled. The captain, Annike, and Xi apparently had not been invited, Marqus realized, as Naseem rapped his avatar's knuckles on the table. "Is it hot in here, or is it just me?" he asked. He let the question hang, then popped a chart into their minds: internal temperature after the deceleration burn. A blue line showed the captain's estimated temperature, and the observed temperature was marked in red. The red line stood higher than the blue from the start, and the gap had widened. "The captain lied to us."

Sonoma said, "So his calculations were off–"

"It's not the calculation." Naseem forced another image into their heads, the *Coronado*. Cracks marred the ceramic insulator, like wrinkles on someone overdue for telomere repair. "I've looked at the insulation the past two days. It's damaged."

"Damaged? How?" Ludmilla asked.

"Maybe turbulence during deceleration." Naseem looked at Marqus. "Or maybe the captain hired a cheap contractor at New Liberia."

Marqus stared back. "How hot will it get?"

"Too hot," Naseem said, and the chart returned to Marqus' mind. The red and blue lines climbed to the upper right. The red line topped 108° in two days, 122° in two days more. "As more heat passes, the cracks worsen."

"We'll be fine," Marqus said. "We have enough water, and the crash tanks have climate control."

"The crash tanks can't handle that much heat. In five days we'll suffer heat stroke. In six we'll be dead. If the deut pellets haven't melted first."

In a blink, Garcia and Annike manifested near Naseem. The captain glared, hands on his hips. "What's going on?"

Naseem puffed out his chest. "You damn well know. Five days from now we'll boil like lobsters."

"Based on your fictional damage assessment?"

"It's the truth!"

Garcia shook his head, then looked at the crew. "He wants you to think it's the truth."

"If Naseem's lying, why are we heating up faster than predicted?" Heinrich asked.

Garcia blinked a few times. "Predictions can be a little off. The heating rate won't get worse. Come on, have I ever endangered you?" He looked around the room, his face confident. At his side, though, Annike looked down, and pressed her lips together.

"I'm calling for a vote under the bylaws," Naseem said. "To declare an emergency over the captain's authority. Your 52% won't count," he told Garcia. "Three-fourths of the remaining shares are needed to win. Given the situation, I move for a vote at the minimum time, eight hours from now."

"I second," Ludmilla said.

Naseem pointed at the captain. "And you can't transfer shares to your supporters before then."

Garcia's eyes narrowed. "I know the rules." He faded out.

Everyone else, save Marqus and Naseem, winked out too. Naseem glanced with a smirk at the space where the captain had been. Marqus stood and propped himself with his fists on the table. "Why are you doing this?"

"Why? He's trying to kill us."

"So your numbers say. How did you calculate them?"

Naseem leaned forward. "My numbers are right. Hell, why am I trying to persuade you? You only have 2%."

"You need 36% out of 48%," Marqus said. "Just 10% more will block you. Annike holds 18%–"

Naseem laughed. "Christ, Marq, she's a lock. So's Xi."

His name wasn't *Marq*, dammit. "We'll see if they're locks in eight hours." Marqus left the Virtual. A private one formed around him; a swank hotel room, on the lowest level of New Liberia's biggest habitat, with diamond windowpanes in the floor. The habitat rotated, carried the window away from Titan. The rings came into view, a glittering line slicing Saturn in half. Marqus slumped on a red velour sofa and thought.

Naseem must be lying. Marqus thought his way into the ship's memory and tracked down the observed temperatures so far. They agreed with Naseem's report. Marqus thought about the thermometers around the ship, but their limited memories agreed as well. Naseem couldn't have falsified all the data.

How had he extrapolated the continued overheating? Marqus' software assistant borrowed insights from the ship's library and assembled models deep in his mind. He felt the models run, but he couldn't tell what the answer would be. He'd have to wait till they finished.

Yet why would Naseem lie? Fear for his own safety, despite the evidence? Possible, yes–

Was Naseem a Preser agent?

That devious raghead–but it made no sense. If Naseem were a Preser agent, why would he want to leave so soon? The Presers didn't yet know the *Coronado* had deviated from its flight plan. If they left now, they'd reach Venus before the Presers knew what they carried.

Unless they knew the *Coronado* had dived the sun. But how? Every message had gone through the censor program on its way to the transmitter. No, Naseem wasn't a spy.

Marqus' models finished. They disagreed widely about how hot it would get. The disagreements revolved around how rapidly the insulation degraded. Naseem had reported the most pessimistic projection, of course, but did he have a reason to be so pessimistic?

He had said he had data about the insulation. He must have given one of the ship's robots a thermometer and guided it, probably by remote-jolting its pleasure and pain circuits, along the hull. He could've guided the robot outside, too… no, the hull was too hot now–

Marqus jolted to the edge of the sofa. The exterior hadn't been too hot before the ship entered solar orbit. Not to measure temperatures, but for something worse. Someone could have guided a robot to the radio transmitters and used it to activate the manual override. Someone could have used a robot to send a message before they dove the sun.

The Presers might have known Garcia's plan for two weeks. They could be in a more distant solar orbit right now, waiting to ambush the *Coronado* on her way to Venus.

He took the stairs two at a time to the door. Down the hall, the Virtual melted away around him, and the floor's curve grew steeper; his attention returned to his body as he ran down the main corridor to the captain's office. His software assistant digested the transmitter access hatch's log, and popped the final result into his consciousness: eight times the hatch had opened–in four pairs of openings a few minutes apart–while the ship traveled from New Liberia to the sun. He knocked on the captain's door.

"What is it, Marqus?" Garcia sounded irritated.

"It's important, sir. We may have a spy on board."

He blinked and found his awareness in his avatar seated in a Virtual of Garcia's office, across the desk from the captain. "Tell me."

"I realized someone could send a robot out to the transmitters. I checked the hatch log. Looks like a robot went out four times, for long enough each time to use the transmitter overrides to send a message."

Garcia's expression hardened. "God damn it."

"I don't know if any messages were sent, though."

"I'm sure there were. Damn traitor. But we'll find the bastard out."

Marqus frowned. "How?"

"During the refit at New Liberia, I added locator tags to the robots. Implants under their skin. It helped the ship's computers guide them through the refit process faster. Afterward I left the tags in. Don't tell anyone."

"I won't." Privacy was difficult to come by; the crew wouldn't be happy if they knew Garcia monitored their robot use. Security came first, though. "So we'll know which robots went to the transmitters."

The captain nodded. "Plus we can tell where they went inside the ship."

The spy would have tied a retransmitter on a robot to get his message sent. He would have been too smart to do that in view of the public cameras. However: "We can infer who might have met them privately." Marqus sensed his subconscious access the camera data and work on it.

"Exactly." The captain nodded. "Marqus, I'm glad you thought of this possibility. Even if no one sent messages through the transmitter override, you've proved yourself. I can't do it now, but as soon as the vote is over, I'll double your share."

Marqus' breath caught. Call it 5000 tons, at 6000 sols per ton... with that much money, he could buy a high-rise apartment in New New York! "I, sir, thank you."

Garcia smiled and waved lazily, as if thirty million sols were nothing. But then his smile melted, and his hand fell to the desk.

A strong conviction, well beyond reasonable doubt, bloomed in Marqus' mind. One robot had gone out the hatch to the transmitter three times. For a few hours before and during the robot's first trip out, Annike had remained in her cabin. Before first going out, the robot spent twenty minutes alone with her.

The conference room–the real one–smelled sweaty. Naseem stood near the table, and people conversed in clumps along the walls. The captain shook hands, but he looked worn and his voice sounded flat. Marqus wondered if he could cope with a lover's treachery as well as Garcia did. People noticed Garcia's demeanor, and whispered among themselves. Sonoma glanced from the captain to Annike and her eyes widened. She went to Garcia and laid her hand on his upper arm. He turned to her with surprise on his features, and the surprise soon turned pleasant.

A throat cleared behind Marqus. "How are you voting?" Ludmilla asked.

"You'll find out."

Her eyelids flashed. "For Garcia? You can't be serious."

"Why not?"

"We already have a hundred thousand tons in the hold. Why take more chances?"

"All we have are Naseem's made-up numbers–"

"Has Garcia refuted them?"

Marqus jerked his head. "No." Garcia wouldn't endanger them. He wouldn't. "But I trust him."

Naseem rapped his gavel. "This meeting is now in order." Chairs squeaked as people sat. Garcia and Sonoma took adjacent seats. The captain looked past her for a moment and caught Marqus' gaze. The gavel rapped again. "The first order of business is the vote."

"No," Marqus said. "Ship's security comes first."

"You stalling?" Naseem asked, then looked at Garcia. "This a trick?"

The captain glanced over. "Marqus?"

"I have evidence Annike Olson has betrayed us to the Presers."

Murmurs erupted. The captain shut his eyes. Olson, seated near Naseem, folded her arms and looked down her nose at Marqus. "Where did you get that idea?"

"You sent a robot out the hatch to the transmitter. Three times." The fourth time must have been a software glitch. None of the ship's robots had gone out then.

Olson shrugged. "Fine, Marqus, you found me out."

Garcia slammed his palm against the tabletop. "Goddammit, Annike! How could you? Betraying me–us–to the Preservationists!"

Her eyes narrowed. "I didn't talk to the Presers!"

Marqus leaned forward. "Of course you would say that."

She turned a sharp gaze on him, which softened when she sagged out a breath. "I'll give you access to all my personal files. You're sharp enough that you'll find if I talked to the Presers."

Garcia's face was tight with leashed anger. "If it wasn't the Presers, who'd you talk to?"

"A Venus futures broker."

The anger came out. "You risked our necks to make a profit?"

"The same profit you could've made if you'd listened to me! I sold 20,000 tons of helium for next month delivery at 6117 sols per ton. You could've sold 50,000 tons! You could have paid off your loan on the *Coronado*."

"You'll bring the Presers down on us!"

"You know I encrypted the messages. Don't get sanctimonious, you know the Preser risk didn't stop you from selling short! Greed did! 'Why sell short?' " She mimicked his voice. " 'The sky's the limit! The cash price will hit 10,000!' If the bubble doesn't burst." She shook her head. "I finally realized I can't stop you from taking foolish risks. But by God I won't take those risks alongside you any more."

Marqus sensed the room's sympathies shift toward Annike, but Garcia's face stayed firm. "Didn't you tell the crew about your scheme? If the bubble burst, didn't you want anyone else to make millions?"

She spread her hands, palms-up, on the table. "I concealed myself as best I could, and you still found me out." She pointed with her chin at Marqus. "If I'd talked to people, someone would have told you. If they had, you would've shut me down. You can't know someone's loyalties, when push comes to shove." She shrugged, and sank into her chair. "Time to vote."

"If no one objects," Naseem said. "We vote in order, highest percentage first. Annike, you have 18%."

"I vote to overrule the captain and depart now."

"Xi, 10%."

"I side with the captain."

Naseem squinted. "Why?" Annike asked.

Xi blinked at her. "Wrong of you to betray your man."

The captain needed just 2% more. As Naseem, Ludmilla, and Raveena voted against the captain, people glanced at Marqus. With his 2%, he could swing the balance the captain's way, and preserve the ship from mutiny. Yet should he? Garcia had led him to suspect Annike, when her only sin had been locking in a profit. What if the helium price bubble had burst while the sun's radio output cut them off from news? What if Naseem was right? He'd trusted the captain; trusted more than he should.

"Sonoma, you have 2.3%."

She nodded, and her face furrowed. "For the captain." She puckered her mouth and frowned at Annike. "You didn't tell us because you just thought about yourself."

Garcia smiled with gratitude as he stared at the back of Sonoma's head. Marqus, though, saw her face, ugly with the worst womanish sneer he'd ever seen. His attraction for her suddenly evaporated, and he wondered why he hadn't seen her real self before.

The meeting crumbled into raised voices and private glances, until Garcia cleared his throat. "I thank the crew for its support," he said. "There do appear to be some discrepancies between the insulation's predicted performance and the actual. So, in the interests of safety, we will leave the chromosphere in 24 hours." He pushed back his chair and left. Sonoma darted after him. Voices returned to full volume, but Marqus said nothing, aware of Annike further up the table and wanting to avoid her. He slipped out.

The air grew thicker as the day passed. The crew didn't stir, and Garcia shut himself in his quarters. Everyone scorned Sonoma and Xi, and they too left the public spaces. Xi stayed in his cabin, with only bubbling solvents audible in the corridor outside. No one could find Sonoma, but when Annike moved into a cabin near the crew quarters it became clear. Sonoma had taken up with the captain.

The ship still sucked in helium; about 130,000 tons, all told. Over thirty million sols for Marqus. Sweat salted his lips and dripped from his chin. He daydreamed of an air-conditioned apartment half a mile above a crowded Earth city.

When the departure time approached, the crew gathered in the main lounge to climb into the crash tanks. People joked and laughed, relieved at the impending burn. "This heat is too much," Heinrich said. "A few more minutes and I'd strip naked."

From her tank, Raveena said innocently, "Wait, captain, I've changed my mind...."

The lids closed on Heinrich's chortle and a chorus of laughs. The mask covered Marqus' face, and gel flowed over him. The captain planned a one gee burn, but turbulence could toss them around.

Marqus watched the bridge through the ship's cameras. The bridge stretched forty feet, long enough to see the floor curve up. Video monitors and speakers covered one wall, and four chairs sprouted from the other wall. The chair backs faced the floor.

Xi stood with folded arms. A monitor's glow lit his face. He wore dungarees and a baggy vest, and sweat dewed on his forehead. How could he stand the heat? Garcia and Sonoma stood in a far corner; her fingers traced the captain's ear.

"Time to burn," Garcia said. After a few seconds the floor loosed its grip on their feet. Rotation had stopped. The captain used a hand-hold to pull himself toward a chair. "Everyone below's in the tanks. Sonoma, Xi, strap in."

Sonoma took the chair at the left end, next to Garcia. Annike and Xi filled the chairs to the right. The straps crawled over their bodies and hooked together. Sudden weight tugged at their faces and pulled them deeper into the chairs. The *Coronado* accelerated away from the sun.

Over the next hour, the gas around the ship thinned, and the sun's chatter over the radio grew a little quieter. Marqus looked through the ship's fore view, and his face felt cool. The ions faded to show a dark gray point sixty-five million miles away. Four days to the SPF-Infinity–

"There's radio interference," Annike said.

Garcia nodded. By now they should hear broadcasts, but instead a droning sound filled all channels. "That's artificial."

–Presers!– Raveena said. The image entered Marqus' mind: a ship resembling a lumpy pyramid of giant balls, the base lit by exhaust from a fusion drive. A Preservationist warship, course and speed so well-matched with the *Coronado* it seemed under tow. "Half a million miles away."

Garcia glared at Annike. "Goddammit, woman! They eaves-dropped on your message to your broker–"

"Maybe they saw the probe! Does it matter? Let's deal with this!"

The radio drone cut off, and a man's voice boomed. "Vessel *Coronado*, registry number november-echo-alpha-niner-eight-foxtrot, this is Jupiter Satellite Union Ship *Rachel Carson*." Marqus turned down the volume. "You are under arrest for transporting helium to the Republic of Venus. You have five minutes to surrender. Failure to do so will be construed as an admission of guilt, and the use of force will be authorized. JSUS *Rachel Carson* out."

Silence filled the bridge, but the crew shouted through the thoughtspace. Then Garcia spoke, voice firm and cold. "No way in hell do we surrender. Traitor, whoever you are, however you warned them, you guessed wrong. If I die, so do you."

"That's crazy!" Xi said. "Better to cut our losses and live on–"

"After they rebuild our personalities?"

"At least it's living! We'd be free, we could be reunited with our families and friends."

"Xi, we're fine. We won't surrender," Garcia said. "We're fast and nimble–"

"Not as fast as a warship!"

"Fast enough. Xi, don't worry, we'll evade them. They're not that powerful. All they have are lasers and fusion bombs. We've just braved a star."

Xi reached into his vest and pulled out a homemade pistol with a dull steel muzzle and a compressed air canister. His free hand grasped his wrist, but still the muzzle shook over Garcia and Annike. "We will surrender."

–We have to do something!– Raveena said privately. –I'm going to the bridge. Who else?–

Marqus didn't hesitate. –Me.– He thought the gel to liquid and opened his tank. Raveena stood, and gel dripped from her bangs and her shorts. Marqus swung his feet to the floor. Doubt tugged him. "I can tweak the cameras between here and the bridge. We can surprise him. But then what?"

Her fists clenched, then relaxed. "One of the reasons I do martial arts–"

"Have you ever fought someone?"

"Do we have a choice?"

On the bridge, Annike's face grew pallid. The captain smirked at the pistol. "What the hell's that?"

"It shoots darts of a rapid tranquilizer. If you're both unconscious, I'll be left in command. Surrender now or I'll use it." Xi's gaze jerked to Annike. "If you try to reconfigure the command structure, I'll use it. It'll knock you out before you can reprogram anything."

Marqus ran up the corridor behind Raveena. Could he reprogram the command structure? No, Garcia had it locked up tight; Marqus needed a minute or more to fix it.

"Look, Xi," the captain said.

"Time's up! We surrender!"

Raveena tiptoed onto the bridge, and Marqus followed. Xi swept the muzzle over Garcia, Annike, and Sonoma. The latter glanced up at Marqus. He raised his finger to his lips. Raveena circled to the right. Xi wouldn't see her over the camera, but if he heard her footsteps... Sonoma's gaze flicked over them. She raised her eyebrow, then leaned toward Xi.

"Gah!" Marqus screamed and jumped at Xi from the left. The navigator spun in his chair, jerked the muzzle toward Marqus, and–

Howled in agony. Raveena's hand descended again, and this time Marqus saw the blow. Her hand slammed into Xi's. Bones cracked, and the pistol clattered to the floor. Xi howled again. His right forearm bent midway between the elbow and wrist, broken by Raveena's first blow. Then Xi cut off his screams, and unclasped himself with his good hand. His gaze locked on the pistol.

Marqus dove for it, rolled onto his side, and fired. The dart caught Xi two inches below his left clavicle. His face grew dreamy, and in moments he sagged back.

"You two have just doubled your shares," the captain said. "Everyone, stay strapped in!"

"What about–" Raveena said.

"Get Xi out. One of you take his chair. The other, shit. Not enough time to get into a crash tank."

Marqus unbuckled Xi. "It's yours," he said.

"You got us here without Xi seeing."

"You landed the blow. I'll ride it out."

Twelve seconds remained on the ultimatum, and a few seconds more would pass before they'd see the Presers' response. Marqus curled up in the corner, forearms over his head. Five seconds, zero, plus five–

Garcia gyrated the ship. The walls slammed into Marqus, and pushed against him with bruising force. The ship accelerated at four gees. He numbed his pain, and watched the ship through an external view cobbled together from internal data and educated guesswork. A few puffs of dust appeared; gamma ray laser impacts. He looked closer. Foot-deep gouges scarred the hull.

–How many shots can we take?– Marqus asked through the thoughtspace. He was short of breath and fearful of biting his tongue if he spoke aloud.

"They'd have to hit the same spot two or three times to pierce the hull." Garcia's voice labored against the acceleration. "Won't happen."

"It won't?" Annike said. She popped the math into everyone's head: if the Presers stayed with them for four days, the Coronado had just a 60.03% chance to reach Venus. "They're closing," she added.

Garcia gritted his teeth. "I'm taking the engines to full power."

"We're at full power, Rey."

"Full safe power. I'll feed deut into the drive at max rate. God willing the injectors won't melt."

"That's 11 gees!" Sonoma said. "The gel can't handle that! People might get strokes."

Garcia glared at her. "We'll throw them in a medtank once we shake the Presers." An image appeared in their minds. The gamma ray laser had taken a chunk from the stern four feet from a previous hit. "Everyone get in crash gel! Everyone but me." He dropped the acceleration to two gees, but slewed the ship even more violently.

Marqus staggered to his feet. He couldn't move his right arm. Raveena unbuckled, her brows knit. "How are you?"

"A broken arm and a few bruises. I'll be fine."

"We need to get to the lounge–"

"They're breaking off!" Annike said. "They stopped firing!"

Marqus looked. The Preser ship veered off and cut acceleration. It shrank with each moment.

"Bastards!" Garcia shouted. He patched in the Preservationist ship for his next words. "You should've known better than to try catching me!"

Marqus leaned against the wall, and his heart slowed. They'd done it! They were rich!

The Preser spoke. "The Jupiter Satellite Union no longer seeks your arrest. JSUS *Rachel Carson* out." The radio jamming ended, and silence roared in their ears. In came all the messages they had missed.

Premier Zhao's negotiations had yielded results: Venus and the Jupiter Satellite Union reached a settlement. The Presers returned to their traditional ban on helium mining from Jupiter's atmosphere. But Venus had compromised too. Construction on the second cooling tower ceased. The market reacted to the news before the Preser ship broke off. Marqus thought for a moment the helium price quote had lost the final digit. No. The price dropped below 500 sols per ton. Garcia frantically called a broker to sell. The order filled at 388¾.

Over the next days, creditors announced foreclosure on the ship. Sonoma moved out of Garcia's cabin, but no one showed her sympathy. "You're why we didn't leave the sun in time," Ludmilla said, and the others agreed. Xi had been dumped into a medtank and sedated, until he could be expelled from the ship when it reached the SPF-Infinity.

With the captain in isolation and Annike, he was certain, still mad at him, Marqus looked into how Xi had sent messages to the Presers. He overrode the lock on Xi's door and looked inside his cabin. To the left stood a large bed, unmade on one side. Tools and parts littered the room, and from the ceiling jutted a desk. The machinery that moved it from the rotation-wall to the thrust-wall must have jammed, and the tools all spilled. A whisking sound came from the other side of the desk. Marqus stooped under the desk, and looked up in surprise.

A small robot hung in the corner, feet splayed on the desk and the ceiling, eyes closed, with a power cable running from its belly to a wall socket. It scrambled awake and disconnected itself, then jumped to the furthest corner and peered at Marqus with a wary and confused look. Xi must have built it without anyone knowing. *That's* what went out the hatch the fourth time. Marqus left the cabin with a smile.

The smile soon faded, though, and it took a while to realize why. He'd been ducking the real issue.

One morning, he used a checkup on his arm as an excuse to stay in the infirmary and think. The only noise came from cooling fans. Through a medtank window, Xi's face looked content. A trick of the drugs? Or did he dream of ending six months' loneliness and reuniting with his wife and daughter?

Belonging. Marqus faced the question: should he go back to New Liberia? Even with the collapse in helium prices, he had earned five million sols; the interest could pay for a five-room apartment, maybe even with a window. He'd had enough adventure. If Xi and Garcia had been his own kind, would they have fooled him?

The door slid open, and Annike walked in. Purple puffs lay under her eyes. "Marqus, how's your arm?"

"Fine." She wasn't surprised to see him here, which meant she'd sought him. He put Xi's tank between them. "I'm leaving–"

"No. Please. We need to talk. I got angry when you caught me."

He took an unsteady breath, but shrugged. "I would've been angry too." He rushed on. "At the meeting, you convinced me. I would have voted against the captain."

"Really?" She thought a moment, shrugged. "Nice to know, but it doesn't change my mind. I'm glad Rey hired you. You proved your worth to the ship."

He winced. "I should've found Xi."

"None of us would have. It's not your fault."

He tapped the navigator's tank with his fingers. "What happens when we reach Venus?"

"The mortgage company will auction off the *Coronado*."

"We'll be unemployed." Maybe he could play tourist for a week or two, before returning to Titan to face his father's gloating.

Annike smiled. "Not you. If you want a job."

"What do you mean?"

"I'm buying a ship. A passenger liner. Lower yield, but lower risk. Raveena already signed on. What do you say? You need time, I'm sure." She stepped back. "We'll have weeks at Venus–"

"I'm in."

"Seriously, take your time."

He probed it, but the sudden conviction held firm. He'd left New Liberia because he didn't belong. Five million sols wouldn't change that. "I took enough time... Captain Olson."

"Officer du Bois." They shook hands and laughed. "I'm heading to the galley. Hungry?"

He looked at a medtank. Did he want to reconfigure his mind? "Yeah, I'll go with you." Even if he needed to, it could wait until after lunch. He had plenty of time to enamor himself of women who wore baggy jumpsuits and practiced *jeet kune do*.

About the Author

Raymund Eich files patent applications, earned a Ph.D., won a national quiz bowl championship, writes science fiction and fantasy, and affirms Robert Heinlein's dictum that specialization is for insects. In a typical day, he may talk with biochemists, electrical engineers, patent attorneys, epileptologists, and rocket scientists. Hundreds of papers cite his graduate research on the reactions of nitric oxide with heme proteins.

Connect with the author at **www.raymundeich.com** or scan the QR code below.

Sign up for his mailing list to receive exclusive, pre-release content about his upcoming books. Your email address will never be shared and you can unsubscribe at any time. Go to **www.raymundeich.com/mailing-list** or scan the QR code below.

OTHER BOOKS BY THE AUTHOR

Available wherever books are sold.

Learn more about these titles at our website, **www.cv2books.com**, or scan the QR code below.

Stone Chalmers

Earth barely survived the 21st Century. Biotechnological and nuclear terrorism, civil war, famine, and ethnic cleansing killed billions. Thousands fled on warpdrive ships to colonize planets around distant suns.

In the 22nd century, after the United Nations established control over Earth, it opened wormhole links to the distant colonies, to prevent a repeat of the previous century's chaos on a galactic scale.

Enter operative Stone Chalmers. Spy. Assassin. Instrument maintaining the UN's order on the settled galaxy.

Opposing him are hostile forces on colony worlds... and within the UN itself.

When Stone clashes with those forces, the UN—and every human world—will be transformed forever.

Learn more about the Stone Chalmers series at **www.cv2books.com/stone-chalmers**, or scan the QR code below.

The Progress of Mankind (#1)

To maintain order in the 22nd century, the UN relocates undesirables through artificial wormholes onto colony planets. Everyone benefits... except the planets' original colonists.

Now, the newly rediscovered colony of New Moravia learns the UN's plan and fights back.

The Greater Glory of God (#2)

Thousands fled the chaos of the 21st century on rogue warpdrive ships to settle colony planets. When Earth reunified in the 22nd, its fleets rediscovered the colonies and hunted down the warpdrive ships.

Every warpdrive ship but one.

To All High Emprise Consecrated (#3)

After unifying Earth, the UN has rediscovered the colony of Minerva. Prosperous and technologically advanced, Minerva quickly submits to UN supremacy.

Surprisingly quickly…

In Public Convocation Assembled (#4)

After unifying Earth, the UN controls all human colonies scattered through the galaxy by means of wormholes, warpdrive ships, and ruthless operatives. Operatives working to strengthen the UN.

Or destroy it.

The Confederated Worlds

The purpose of all other combat arms is to put the infantryman in sole possession of the battlefield.

A thousand years from now, while Earth sleeps in virtual reality, three polities—the Confederated Worlds, the Unity, and the Progressive Republic—strive to connect the scattered, terraformed worlds of humankind by artificial wormholes. When they meet, they clash, in a decades-long struggle of arms that will embroil every human world, in which dedication to duty liberates worlds—and oneself.

Learn more about the Confederated Worlds series at **www.cv2books.com/the-confederated-worlds**, or scan the QR code below.

Take the Shilling (Book 1)

The Confederated Worlds implanted in his brain the skills to make him a soldier. Tomas Neumann had to learn for himself how to survive interstellar war.

Operation Iago (Book 2)

The Confederated Worlds lost the war. Can Lt. Tomas Neumann win the peace against elusive, deceptive foes out to turn the Confederated Worlds against itself?

A Bodyguard of Lies (Book 3)

Assigned to the halls of power, only Capt. Tomas Neumann can save the Confederated Worlds from the ultimate treachery.

Novels

The Blank Slate

Neuroscience entrepreneur Clay Shieffer must stop a tyrannical president... because he unwittingly gave the tyrant power over the human mind.

New California

After New California's founder committed suicide, two men vied to rule the colony.

Ashwin George, supported by the colony's elite and the Chinese company dominating half the settled galaxy.

Against him, Desmond Park, nanotechnology engineer, armed with the most formidable weapon of all.

A single idea.

Short Novels

The ALECS Quartet

He had a month to learn the planet's mysteries—and Juliette's.

His cover story: return to Elard to dismantle his sect's missionary work to the planet's natives.

His true mission: investigate decades-old mysteries of love and death.

His objective: return to Earth with his discovery.

If he can.

Collections

The First Voyages: The Complete Science Fiction Stories 1998-2012

From 21st century asteroid settlements to World War II Romania, from an Earth dominated by immortal aliens to Christ's empty tomb, a fresh, distinctive voice in science fiction will take you on journeys to the photosphere of the sun, the coding regions of DNA, and the complexities of the human psyche.

www.ingramcontent.com/pod-product-compliance
Lightning Source LLC
Chambersburg PA
CBHW051928220626
47052CB00003B/627